Picnic Farm

For Catherine and Ellen - love, Christine.

For my fabulous parents - all my love, Sarah.

First published 1998 by Macmillan Children's Books
This edition published 1998 by Macmillan Children's Books
a division of Macmillan Publishers Limited
20 New Wharf Road, London N1 9RR
Basingstoke and Oxford
Associated companies througout the world
www.panmacmillan.com

ISBN 0 333 68361 7

3 5 7 9 8 6 4

A CIP catalogue record for this book
is available from the British Library.

Printed in China

Picnic Farm

Christine Morton and Sarah Barringer

MACMILLAN CHILDREN'S BOOKS

Here are the children at the farm.

Here is the farmer showing them round,

and these are the things they saw...

A sheep, a sheep – a shy old sheep.

A hen, a hen—a squabbling hen.

Trees, trees-tall fruit trees.

Bees, bees - buzzing bees.

A cow, a cow—a chewing cow.

A churn, a churn - a turning churn.

Wheat, wheat-waving wheat.

Grass, grass—good green grass.

Here are the children out in the yard.

Here is the farmer leading the way,

and these are the things they brought...

A rug, a rug - of wool from the sheep.

Eggs, eggs-laid by the hen.

Plums, plums - picked from the trees.

honey

Honey, honey-made by the bees.

Milk, milk-milked from the cow.

Butter, butter—made in the churn.

Bread, bread-made from the wheat.

And a chocolate cake
that the children made!

Here is the stream they sat beside.

They ate and they ate and they ate and they ate . . .

...and they all fell asleep

on the good green grass.